CHILLERS

FIRE RAISER

Philip Wooderson

Illustrated by
Jane Cope

A & C Black · London

CHILLERS
The Day Matt Sold Great-grandma, Eleanor Allen
Ghost from the Sea, Eleanor Allen
Sarah Scarer, Sally Christie
Hide and Shriek! Paul Dowling
Clive and the Missing Finger, Sarah Garland
Madam Sizzers, Sarah Garland
Jimmy Woods and the Big Bad Wolf, Mick Gowar
Ghost Riders, Alex Gutteridge
The Real Porky Philips, Mark Haddon
The Nearly Ghost Baby, Delia Huddy
The Haunting of Nadia, Julia Jarman
Wilf, the Black Hole and the Poisonous Marigold,
    Hiawyn Oram
The Blob, Tessa Potter
The Dinner Lady, Tessa Potter
Freak Out!, John Talbot
Spooked, Philip Wooderson
The Mincing Machine, Philip Wooderson
Fire Raiser, Philip Wooderson

First published in Great Britain 1997 by
A & C Black (Publishers) Ltd
35 Bedford Row, London WC1R 4JH

Copyright © 1997 Philip Wooderson
Illustrations © 1997 Jane Cope
Philip Wooderson and Jane Cope have asserted their moral
rights to be identified respectively as the author and illustrator
of this work.

ISBN 0-7136-4783-3

Set in 15/18 pt Meridien by Dalia Hartman, London.
Printed and bound in Great Britain by
William Clowes (Beccles) Ltd, Beccles and London.

Chapter One
Fags & Mags

Mrs Bizzle is a nasty
old crone, but it's her son,
Spike-the-Bike, who really
gives me the shivers. Even the
lollipop lady has to get out of his way.

Spike rides his bike at scrambles.
He brings it home covered in
mud and takes it to bits in
his yard. Then he puts it
back together, polishes
it until it gleams; then
goes scrambling again.

Spike is out to get me. He thinks I stuck chewing gum on his saddle.

I didn't.
It was Denny.
I bet you.

Mum and Dad are always telling me to stay away from the Bizzles. I wish I could, but today I just *had* to go into their creepy old shop.

RAGS & MAGS

clang-a-lang-a-lang

As I opened the door, a bell jangled deep in the gloom.

4

Something furry brushed my leg. The air reeked of rotting fish and cats' pee. A cat crouched on one of the shelves and another one was stretched out on the counter right next to what I'd come for.

PREMIER LEAGUE FOOTBALL STICKERS

I only had five spaces left to fill in my football album. Three or four days ago my nearest rival, Denny, still had sixteen stickers to collect.

But this afternoon Denny had been boasting he only needed nine more. So, I was desperate for stickers – not in three days when I got my pocket money, but right now. I'd have to spend my birthday money. Mum would not be pleased.

I picked up the nearest packet and held it up to the light, trying to see through the wrapper, but—

PUT 'EM BACK!
DON'T LIKE THIEVES
IN HERE!

Mrs Bizzle must have moved fast. She'd popped up out of nowhere. And now she was blinking at me through her dusty old specs and smiling a horrible smile as if her mouth were melting.

I pulled out my ten pound note. She snatched it, saying, "I've just caught one of your school friends trying to pinch stickers."

I told him Spike would make him sorry.

Before I could ask her which "friend", something roared up the street, making the whole shop rattle.

Oh, no. It's SPIKE!

Mrs Bizzle, quick! Can I pay for three packets?

Too late. Spike burst into the shop, stinking of petrol fumes. He was wearing a greasy string vest, and black leather trousers and boots. He was big and hefty, his pale face speckled with huge red spots like an under-cooked cherry cake.

7

He pushed me
aside so
he could get
at the till.

> Out of the
> way squirt.

HEY!

> I need money.
> Rear strut's gone
> again, Mum.

> But–
> Spiky, we've got
> no money.

"Just need another ten quid,"
he said, grabbing my ten pound note
out of her hand! He didn't even say thank
you. I yelled—

> It's mine.
> Give it
> back!

His
nostrils
flared.

SNIFF
SNIFF

> What's that?

But he wasn't talking to me.

Spike yanked aside a grubby grey
curtain, revealing a grotty room stuffed
to the ceiling with junk. In the corner, a
camp bed heaved with more dozy cats.

"It's out in the yard!" Spike said, and as he lugged the back door open, in rolled a thick cloud of *SMOKE!*

Spike grabbed the phone, stabbed in a number and bawled:

> THERE'S A FIRE IN MY WORKSHOP. BIKES WORTH A—

> Nobody's there! Mum, what—?

> Phone's been cut off.

> Why? Didn't you pay the bill?

Spike gave me such a glare, I took a step back. My feet tangled with something down on the floor. A cat? No. It was a schoolbag. Denny's!

Mrs Bizzle pointed to the door.

> Go on, sweetie. Come back for your money tomorrow.

> Yeah, OUT!

Before I knew what was happening, Spike had booted me out of the shop.

Back home, I couldn't tell Mum I'd lost my ten pounds birthday money, but I told her about the fire. I tried to sound really calm.

> Spike will lose all his bikes. The petrol tanks will explode — probably blow the roof off!

> Yeouch!

> Their phone's out of order, Mum. The fire brigade ought to be called.

CRACK!

"Rubbish," said Dad, coming in with a grin on his face. "I just walked past their yard. It's only Spike burning some old tyres."

But Spike didn't light them.

How do you know?

I heard what he said.

When? Where?

Have you been in that shop, Jarvis? What for?

Football stickers?

Don't joke. He's not THAT stupid. But, as for those horrible Bizzles, you keep clear of them, Jarvis.

I will! Once I've got back what they owe me.

Ummm. What's for tea?

I asked, trying to change the subject.

"Tell you what," Dad said, giving me a wink, "Saturday we'll go shopping to spend your birthday money."

Chapter Two
More Tangled Up

Next morning I felt more hopeful. But when I got to the shop, there was a note on the door.

So, I had to go to school without either stickers or money. And the first thing I saw in the playground was Denny helping himself from one of the juniors.

He flicked a throwaway lighter. The flame shot up half a metre, setting the sticker on fire. I managed a scornful laugh.

But I'm still ahead of you. And I'm not cheating!

YOU TWO! In my study. NOW!

It was our headmaster, Mr Horowitz the Horrible.

Two minutes later we were standing in front of his desk.

I've had a complaint about you boys.

I ain't done nothin'.

H-the-H glared at Denny while lifting a bag from under the desk. "You left this in Fags and Mags. And this." He took out a *Tingle* lemonade bottle and undid the cap.

What does this smell of?

Ugh! A bit like... PETROL.

Spike Bizzle said he found it next to some burning rubbish in his yard. He claims Denny started the fire to get his own back because Mrs Bizzle caught him stealing football stickers!

"I never, Sir! It's a set-up! I hate Spike. And his mother," Denny protested.

H-the-H wagged his finger. "It's lucky we're only talking about some old tyres and rags or you'd be in deep water. As it is, I want that lighter. It's confiscated. And as for you—" H-the-H turned on me.

"What's this about you *acting as decoy*, distracting poor Mrs Bizzle while Denny was starting the fire?"

I stared at him.

"Don't tell me." H-the-H shut his eyes. "Those wretched football stickers! You know I banned swapping them in school."

No loss for Denny, maybe. But I still *had* to go back.

Chapter Three
Kind Mrs Bizzle

After school, the shop was open.
Spike was not around, so I slipped in.

clang-a-lang

But where had the stickers gone?

Mrs Bizzle limped in from the back room.

I've come for—

Spike says he'll bring some more from the storeroom next week.

NEXT WEEK?!
But Mrs Bizzle, it's urgent!

Denny would fill his album before me, and Mum would go ballistic about my birthday money. I'd have to buy stickers somewhere else.

I need my ten pounds back, please.

What a shame — Spike's emptied the till. Why don't you take a few comics, or sweeties, instead.

Mrs Bizzle—

I had a desperate idea. I asked if she'd go and get me ten pounds' worth of stickers from Spike's storeroom so I could sell them at school to get my money back.

Sorry, dearie. It's too far with my poor gammy knee.

Where is it?

Babcock Road. Go there in an hour. Tell Spike I sent you. He'll help.

She couldn't remember which number. But my friend, Carmine, lived in that road so she'd probably know.

Chapter Four
Spike's Scary Storeroom

Carmine's house was
a big, rambling place,
divided into six flats,
with a huge,
overgrown garden.

I rang the bell.
Nobody answered.
But when I pushed
the door it squeaked
back on its hinges.
The lock had been
ripped right off.
Inside, the lights
didn't work. And
someone had sprayed
graffiti all the way up
the stairs. I was glad
when I reached
Carmine's flat.

Carmine was out but her mum said she would be back soon.

Come in and wait. There's fudge cake.

I couldn't say no to fudge cake. While I munched away she told me why the house was in such a terrible state. It was thanks to their *friendly* landlord. He had already forced out the rest of the tenants.

But we're more stubborn, so he's trying even nastier tricks. Like turning off the power and making the boiler play up.

But weren't you all paying him rent?

"Our rents weren't enough for him. He's greedy. He wants to knock the house down so he can make a fortune selling the land for new houses. But—" She chortled. "He can't get planning permission!"

Serves him right, I thought
as I accepted a slice
more fudge cake. Then
Carmine turned up.

> What brings
> you here?

I told her I needed to find
Spike Bizzle's storeroom. This brought
on a funny reaction.

> It's in our basement.

> SPIKE'S basement!
> Seeing as Spike
> is our landlord.

I didn't like this one bit,
especially when Carmine led me
back down the stairs to the front hall and
opened a narrow door under the staircase.

It's scary. From here on, you can lead the way.

Cobwebs plastered my fingers. And when Carmine clicked on a light switch, all I could see was junk and a huge old boiler.

"Spike's storeroom is through that door," said Carmine, pointing.

I twisted the handle and pushed. Much to my surprise, the door wasn't locked.

It opened with a . . .

CREAK!

There was just enough light to show the shelves round the walls. They were laden.

But what was THAT →
doing here?

I picked up the petrol can. Before I could show it to Carmine, I heard—

FLASH - BOOOOOOM!

"Don't panic. It's only the boiler," said Carmine.

It looked as old as the house, and bristled with pipes and dials, all rattling and vibrating and belching poisonous fumes as it started to heat up the water.

> It's LETHAL. One day it'll explode and blow up the house!

Carmine said Spike had mucked up the timer so it came on at odd hours, or didn't come on at all.

> Hhhhhh! Speak of the devil!

I looked round and followed her gaze.

Carmine ducked behind some old boxes, while I backed up against the wall, bumping the petrol can on the brickwork.

23

His fists clenched.
He took a step
closer.

His greasy forehead throbbed and his eyes
bulged as he noticed the can in my hand.

Spike took another step closer, raising his
big blunt hands. I thought I was going to
be strangled. Maybe Carmine did too. At
any rate, she broke cover and made a
dash for the exit.

He reeled round – a moment
too late! All he saw were
her trainers disappearing
up the steps.

I dodged between him and the doorway.
His hand shot out. I bounced sideways
and crash-dived into
a heap of junk.

He tried to grab my ankle.

I kicked out and
sent him sprawling.

This won me a few
vital seconds. I scurried
behind the boiler but it was
so blisteringly hot I squeezed out
the other side as fast as I possibly could.

Covered in cobwebs and soot, I legged
it after Carmine, spurred on by Spike's
angry bellowing.

COME BACK
HERE, YOU
LITTLE TYKE!

Chapter Five
H-the-H Knows Best

I may have escaped strangulation, but I had lost all hope of getting any stickers from Spike. He'd really be out to get me now, EVEN MORE THAN BEFORE. So, what was I to do?

I had a nasty moment when Dad came home from work. Leaning over the banisters I heard him talking to Mum.

. . . poor Bizzles. You can't help feeling sorry for—

Had Spike already told him?

I tiptoed downstairs, my heart thudding, but before I reached the kitchen I heard Mum sounding angry.

"*Poor* Bizzles! Their shop *deserves* to go bust – all those mangy old cats and stale sweets. The sooner it shuts down the better. But they'll have a nasty surprise if they think they can pay their debts by selling the Babcock Road house. It's practically derelict, thanks to that Spike. He's a monster."

Dad was winking again.

He saw me wince.

What's the matter? Not blown it all on football stickers, I hope!

I should be so lucky. The money had been blown on a motorbike part for Spike's Harley Davidson. And if Fags and Mags shut down, it would be lost for ever. It didn't bear thinking about.

But I thought about it . . .

ALL night . . .

£10 . . .

£10!

And going to school in the morning.

When I got to Fags and Mags I saw they *were* closing down. Did that mean the stickers would go too? I felt a twinge of hope, until I opened the door and saw Spike behind the counter.

I took off down the street and didn't stop till I reached the school. And who should I see in the playground but Denny, trading more stickers.

Only five to go now. You haven't got a chance, Jarvis.

Could things get worse than this?
Yes. Carmine rushed up to tell me:

H-the-H wants to see you again!

He didn't *look* pleased to see me.

Spike Bizzle phoned. Claims he caught you in his storeroom with a can of petrol! . . . Denny, too, I gather!

No, I wasn't with Denny.

You mean, the rest IS true?

I took a deep breath and told him I had only gone down there to ask Spike for what he owed me, and how I'd seen the petrol can alongside the two bottles of *Tingle*. "It made me wonder if Spike had tried to frame Denny and me for starting the fire in his yard," I finished.

H-the-H snorted at this. "Jarvis," he said, "Spike's bikes run on petrol. He sells lemonade in his shop. Of course he'd have those things in his storeroom. I still have my doubts about Denny, but one thing's perfectly clear. You'll have to go back to the shop and tell Mrs Bizzle from me . . .

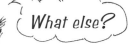

. . . she's to hand back your money, or else!

What else?

I wondered out loud.

H-the-H shuffled his shoes and spoke gruffly.

First, I'll have to tell your parents.

Anything else but that, please!

No need, Sir. I'll sort it out.

I tried to sort it out straight after school. Luckily, Spike wasn't in the shop, so I could tell Mrs Bizzle what H-the-H had said. She opened the till.

All yours, dear.

She counted out 93 pence.

G-R-O-A-N-N-N

No need to be gloomy, sweetie. I think I can probably help you.

I stared at her. How could she help me? If she couldn't give me back my ten pounds, H-the-H would tell my parents what I'd done with my birthday money.

Mrs Bizzle snatched hold of my elbow and pulled me close enough to whisper in my ear.

She gave a little titter.

"Don't go when Spike's around, though," she warned. "Try tomorrow evening, he'll be at a motorbike scramble. And the rest of the building is empty. He's booted out all his tenants."

I nearly said, "Carmine still lives there!" But, instead, I said, "How do I get in?"

Chapter Six
No Smoke Without Fire

It looked like my only chance.

It wasn't the best sort of chance, breaking in like a burglar. But, would I be breaking the law if I only took what I was owed – £9.07 worth of stickers? And Mrs Bizzle *had* as good as told me I could help myself.

That night, I had grisly nightmares about being cornered by Spike. I woke up and tried to calm down by thinking of something less scary. But as soon as I drifted back into sleep, Denny appeared out of nowhere and snatched my football sticker album.

Fire! . . . Smoke! . . .

Cough-cough-cough!

I woke up coughing.
And I could *still*
smell smoke.

Groping my way to the landing I peered
down into the hall. No cracklings or
fizzlings or flames. But there *was* smoke in
the air. Nasty acrid smoke.

I ran into my parents' room and crouched
beside the bed. "Dad?" I hissed, shaking
him urgently. "Wake up! PLEASE!"

*Ummmm. What's
the trouble?*

When I told him,
he only yawned
and said it was
nothing, just
rubbish in
the Bizzles'
yard.

*It's still smouldering,
I expect. Now, off
you go, back to bed.*

I went to my bedroom window. Across two other gardens there was the Bizzles' backyard. The night air was hazy with smoke. But their rubbish heap wasn't just smouldering. It was blazing! Big yellow sparks were weaving up into the sky.

What's more, I saw Spike and his mother, flitting left and right, casting long black shadows. I thought they were feeding the flames, but then I saw Mrs Bizzle was beating the fire with a broom, and Spike had a garden hose.

The flames died down
quite quickly, but the smoke
got thicker and thicker and hung
over the yard, engulfing both the
Bizzles in a great grey swirling fog.

I looked at my watch. Half-past two.
I had the nastiest feeling I would
be hearing more about this.

Chapter Seven
It's a Frame-up

Sure enough, over our cornflakes, the telephone blared.

It's Spike Bizzle!

... I CAUGHT YOUR KID IN MY STOREROOM! AND LAST NIGHT, HE AND DENNY WERE BACK IN MY YARD! I CAN PROVE IT. THEY LEFT ANOTHER TINGLE BOTTLE REEKING OF PETROL. YOU TELL 'IM FOR ME, WHEN I CATCH THEM TWO, THEY'LL WISH THEY'D NEVER BEEN BORN!

Mum slammed down the phone. "The man's crazy."

"In a bad state," Dad suggested, "what with all his debts. He'll be trying to blame Jarvis for *them* next!"

Mum gripped my arm. "Don't worry. You just steer clear of him, darling. If he makes any more trouble we'll call the police."

DON'T WORRY?
I hadn't started that fire, or left the Tingle bottle in the yard. Nor had Denny. I know he's not that bad. It MUST have been Spike.

But could I prove it?

Remember that 3-pack: 3 – 1 – 1 = 1!

Were there two bottles left now or one?

If I got into Spike's storeroom I could see for myself.

Chapter Eight
In Feet First

At school, I was expecting to be hauled in to see the Head again. Spike would surely have phoned him. But H-the-H called for Denny and questioned him until break.

When Denny came out he was seething. "I've been set up. Bet it's your fault. You want to see me done for because I'm filling my album faster than you."

But I'll beat you, Jarvis. I've only got ONE space left!

One space! So do I!

This was desperate.
If Denny won he'd be CROWING.
I'd have to go through with my plan.

That evening,
I scribbled a note.

Then I set off for
Babcock Road,
hoping I'd
be home
again
before
Mum
found
the note.

Carmine's house looked dark and empty.
Her flat was at the back. But, rather than
climb the stairs, I pushed between the
bushes at the side of the house.

My trainers squelched in
mud as I felt along the wall,
up and down, left and right, nearly
poking my eye out on an unfriendly twig.
But I found it. An old iron
shutter on the entrance
to the coal shute, just as
Mrs Bizzle had described.

Now what? Sitting down on the sill, I dangled my legs through the gap and gingerly lowered myself into the dark below. Only when I was safely inside did I dare to pull out my torch.

But before I could flash it around I saw another light through the half-closed doorway that must have led into Spike's storeroom.

Taking a grip on myself I edged up close to the doorway and peered through. Sure enough, the walls were lined with shelves that were crammed with cardboard boxes. And . . .

SOMEBODY WAS IN THERE!

Denny! Stealing stickers! No wonder he caught up so fast!

HEY!

Denny lurched
backwards, dropping
a handful of stickers.
His eyes were like pound
coins. He swung his torch up, saw my
face, and suddenly he was grinning.

Getting your own back, eh, Jarvis? But I got here first, so I beat you!

And off he went,
dodging past me
and legging it out
through the coal hole.

I took a deep breath. Did I care? Not about football stickers. What mattered was finding that three-pack. I flashed my torch round the storeroom.
No sign of it in the corner, nor up on the shelves. It was gone! So was the can of petrol.

I suddenly felt very flat. Perhaps Spike had needed the petrol for the scramble, afterall, and Denny *had* started both fires.

Rustle rustle

Hold on. What's that noise?

It was coming from the boiler room. I pressed my ear to the door. Someone was shuffling about.

46

Chapter Nine
No Way Out

All I could see through
the keyhole were balls
of crumpled paper
piled against the
boiler. But I could
hear sloshing sounds.

gurgle-urgle-urgle
ca-splish-sploshhh

After a second or two,
there was a familiar smell.

PETROL!

I flashed my torch.

It was trickling
under the door, soaking
into cardboard boxes,
spreading out in a horrible
shape like a twisted claw. HELP!

Was Spike going to burn the house down? He'd be able to sell the land then, and pay off his debts! It all fitted. He had been framing Denny and me – setting us up for *THE BIG ONE!*

But now I had caught him at it, I could leg it and phone the police!

I hurried back into the coal hole and did my best to climb out. I gained an easy toehold on a pipe running round the wall.

But the iron shutter was stuck.

I pushed harder.

I gave an enormous shove, lost my balance and toppled down hard on the floor.

As I lay there, taking this in, I heard—

The boiler-room door had opened. Something clattered inside. I'd not got a moment to lose. I rushed back into the storeroom, just as the door swung shut.

The door was smooth on my side.

There was
no handle or catch.

Spike's petrol can lay nearby, on its side.

It was empty!

I yelled.

Then I peered through the keyhole. This time I saw a hand twiddling a dial on the boiler. But it wasn't Spike's. It was much too small.

And it looked too OLD.

Could Mrs Bizzle be out there?

Perhaps she'd followed Spike and caught him sploshing the petrol. But, why would she fiddle with the time switch? Was she trying to stop the boiler from starting?

I squinted. The main switch was still ON. Only the timer arrow had been moved to point at quarter past eight.

Half an hour off.

Why do that?
UNLESS—

There was one explanation.

As soon as the boiler fired up there would be the usual flash. The petrol-soaked paper would catch light and the whole place would go up in flames!

By then, that wicked old woman would be safely back at home, nursing her *gammy* knee. Spike would still be at his scramble. And Denny and I would be blamed!

I screamed.

> MRS BIZZLE! I'M TRAPPED! You must have forgotten. I came for my stickers!

There was no answer.

I peered through the keyhole again, but the light was off now.

She had gone.

Chapter Ten
My Final Countdown

I did a lot more shouting but it
was like being in a dungeon.

The building was
empty except for
Carmine's family.
They would never
hear me, their flat
was too far up. The
first thing they'd
know about it
would be when
the boiler exploded.
They could get
trapped by the flames!

When I next looked at my
watch, fifteen minutes had passed and—

SSSSSSSSSS

It wasn't the boiler. This hiss seemed to be coming from the coal hole. I stumbled towards it, praying Denny had come to his senses and pulled back the bolt.

But the shutter was still firmly in place. The hissing noise came from the mains water pipe running around the wall. The water gushed on and on, as if a bath was filling.

So what? It couldn't help me. And it wouldn't help Carmine, or her mum, unless—

What if I turned off the stopcock?

Easy. The hissing noise stopped.

What will Carmine's mum do, now? Come down and see what's wrong or sit up there cursing Spike for turning off the water again!?

The seconds ticked by, and the minutes. Back at the boiler-room door, all I could hear was the timer, click-click-clicking away; until I was suddenly hoping no one *would* come downstairs, in case they got caught in the fireball.

CLICK!

One minute left.

I flashed my torch round the storeroom. There were muddy footprints and stickers all over the floor.

Chapter Eleven
The Sound of Silence

I wondered if I was dead. But being dead had to be different to breathing in petrol fumes.

And, anyway, I could hear footsteps hurrying down the stairs and someone shouting.

JARVIS! Are you in there?

DAD!

I managed to tell him, by yelling through the keyhole, how I'd slipped in through the coal hole.

Dad soon had
the shutter
unbolted. He
reached down
and dragged
me out.

Then he was hugging me tight, bawling
into my ear that Mum had found my note
and telephoned Carmine's mother who
hadn't a clue where I was. She was scared
of what Spike might do if he found me in
his house again.

Anyway, what **were** you doing?

I did my best to explain things.

. . . Lucky the boiler conked out.

But Dad was an expert on boilers.

You must have switched off the boiler by stopping the water supply.

"If Carmine's mother was running a bath, the boiler would have run dry," he explained, "so the safety valve cut off the starter."

Then Dad looked extra thoughtful. "Amazing the safety valve still worked, considering the state of the thing, but—"

He gave me an extra tight hug.

That's why you're still with us, thank goodness.

GASP!

What do we do now, Dad?

Call the police.

Chapter Twelve
Who Wins in the End?

The police went to Fags and Mags.

Eventually, after a whole lot of muddling, Mrs Bizzle owned up.

Spike's bikes had been the reason the Bizzles had got into debt, but Spike hadn't known his mother was the one starting the fires and planting the bottles of *Tingle*. She had framed Denny and me so we would get the blame when the house in Babcock Road burnt down. Then she could have claimed the insurance without anyone suspecting she had done it herself.

It didn't bear thinking about.

As for my birthday money, Dad slipped me another ten pounds. "You saved Carmine's life, and her family. What's ten pounds compared to that?" he said, giving me a slap on the back.

We're really proud of you, Jarvis.

As for my enemy, Denny, he was a bit shamefaced when we met in the playground next morning. He didn't say sorry exactly. He didn't even own up to shutting the bolt on the coal hole. But he gave me a football sticker.